THE
DORM
ROOM
DIET
PLANNER

DAPHNE OZ

NEWMARKET PRESS  NEW YORK

This book is published in the United States of America.

FIRST EDITION

ISBN: 978-1-55704-761-8

10 9 8 7 6 5 4 3 2 1

Based on Daphne Oz's *The Dorm Room Diet,* published by Newmarket Press in 2006 (ISBN: 978-1-55704-685-7).

Library of Congress Cataloging-in-Publication Data

Oz, Daphne.
  The dorm room diet planner / Daphne Oz. — 1st ed.
    p. cm.
  ISBN-13: 978-1-55704-761-8 (pbk. : alk. paper) 1. College students—Nutrition. 2. College students--Health and hygiene. 3. Weight loss. I. Title.

RA777.3.O92 2006
613'.0434--dc22

2007020842

QUANTITY PURCHASES
Companies, professional groups, clubs, and other organizations may qualify for special terms when ordering quantities of this title. For information or a catalog, write Special Sales Department, Newmarket Press, 18 East 48th Street, New York, NY 10017; call (212) 832-3575; fax (212) 832-3629; or e-mail info@newmarketpress.com.

www.newmarketpress.com

Designed by Kris Tobiassen
Illustrations by Machiko

Manufactured in the United States of America.

CONTENTS

INTRODUCTION

Congratulations! By opening this planner, you've taken a big step toward making the kind of lifestyle changes that will keep you looking good and feeling great not just in college, but for the rest of your life. Making the transition to college life is huge. Suddenly you feel an independence you never knew before, where you're in complete control. You're working hard and playing hard. This major change is a golden opportunity to seize control over your health and your weight. The Dorm Room Diet offers guidelines for creating a healthy lifestyle and gives you the tools to stop using food as an emotional crutch.

You may know me already from *The Dorm Room Diet*, but for those of you who don't, let me tell you a little about myself. I'm a college student. My dad and both of my grandfathers are heart surgeons, my uncle's a neurosurgeon, my grandmother specializes in homeopathic remedies and complementary medicine—oh, and my mom's a vegetarian. But even with all this great knowledge surrounding me, I had a weight problem between the ages of seven and seventeen. At my heaviest, I was about 30 pounds over-weight. I started making big changes in high school. By the time I got to college, I not only managed to skip the dreaded Freshman 15 but *lost* 10 pounds and became healthier than I'd ever been. I wrote *The Dorm Room Diet* because all my friends wanted to know how I lost the weight and kept it off, and the companion book you are holding is an interactive guide to help you do the same. Trust me, I know you can do this.

Since my first book came out, I've received so many posi-tive comments and e-mails from readers telling me how helpful they found the Dorm Room Diet—not just because it provides them with the basic knowledge they need to take control of their health, but also because it gives them the tools and strate-gies to make the necessary changes. Most important, readers across the nation have found the tips to be easily applicable to life on a college campus.

The first part of *The Dorm Room Diet Planner*, "Get Inspired," helps you take the first steps toward more conscious, healthy eating. In "Get Informed," you'll get a short course in nutrition that will help you choose the right foods to get your health back on track. And it's full of tips on how to avoid the Danger Zones specific to college life. "Get Moving" is a great section on exercises you can do even in your little dorm room, complete with logs to track your progress. In "Get the Numbers," I've included a few charts and things about getting the right vitamins and minerals, calculating metabolic rate and activity level, and finding your optimal weight for your height and frame. "Get Going" is a series of daily journal pages for your first thirty days on the Dorm Room Diet. Each day has a kernel of advice or information to help inspire you, and blanks to fill in about your eating, exercise, and stress level that day.

This Planner will give you all the structure you will need to succeed. Good luck! Remember that independence is all about choice: Choose to live a healthy, happy life!

GET
INSPIRED

Fad diets usually lead to failure because their rules can be hard to follow. With the Dorm Room Diet, there are no rules—you're in charge of what, when, where, and how you eat.

Before we get started, read and sign this contract with yourself. Then tear it out and post it on your fridge or tuck it in your wallet. At times when you get frustrated, review it. It will help you remember why you're working so hard.

- -

I agree to commit to improving my nutritional habits and my physical well-being. I am done with fad diets. Instead I'm going to arm myself with the knowledge to make informed decisions. I'll do my best to use food for its purpose as fuel for the body and not as an emotional crutch. I know this won't always be easy. When I slip up I'll brush off the dust and get back on track.

Name _____ Date _____

WHAT'S YOUR EATING STYLE?

Learn to identify when and why you eat the way you do.

How you and your family viewed food while you were growing up will have an enormous impact on how well you adjust to eating in a new setting like college. The first step toward healthy eating is to identify and root out bad habits. So let's create a portrait of how family life influenced the way you feel about food now.

1. HOW MANY MEALS DID YOU EAT PER DAY?

2. HOW REGULAR WERE THESE MEALS?

3. DID YOU EAT SNACKS? If so, were they generally prepackaged or freshly prepared? (nuts, fruits, veggies, and yogurt count as freshly prepared)

4. HOW MANY MEALS, PER DAY, DID YOU EAT WITH ANOTHER PERSON?

5. WOULD YOU SAY THAT YOUR MEALS WERE "RUSHED" OR "RELAXED"?

6. DID YOU REGULARLY EAT WHILE WATCHING TV, talking online or on the phone, or otherwise occupied?

7. HOW MANY MEALS, PER DAY, DID YOU PREPARE FOR YOURSELF?

8. DID YOU HELP PLAN MEALS or did you eat what was put on the table?

9. HOW OFTEN (MEALS PER WEEK) DID YOU EAT IN A RESTAURANT or order takeout? _____

10. DID YOU PREFER HOME-COOKED MEALS or something made outside the home? _____

11. HOW HEALTHFULLY, ON A SCALE OF 1–10, 10 being the most healthy, do you think your family eats? _____

12. ON THE SAME SCALE OF 1–10, how healthfully do you think you eat now? _____

13. WOULD YOU SAY THAT YOU ARE AWARE of what you *should* be eating? If yes, how successful, on a scale of 1–5 (5 being very successful), are you at following these guidelines? _____

14. IF YOU ANSWERED "YES" TO QUESTION 13, please list the source of your information (parents, Internet, teacher, and so on). _____

15. WHAT IS THE SINGLE BIGGEST OBSTACLE to eating healthfully you face? _____

Good habits from home I can build on:

_____

_____

_____

_____

_____

Poor habits I can work to change:

_____

_____

_____

_____

_____

_____

LET'S GET STARTED!

Here are three easy steps you can follow to start eating healthfully right away:

1. DRINK A GLASS (OR TWO) OF WATER BEFORE YOU EAT ANY MEAL.

2. TRY NOT TO EAT WHEN YOU ARE DISTRACTED (watching TV, using the Internet, at parties). The food you are most likely to eat in these settings is probably processed junk anyway, and you'll end up gorging on snacks that won't keep you full. Your goal is to be conscious of what you eat at all times.

3. TRY NOT TO EAT LESS THAN TWO HOURS BEFORE BED. You'll guarantee yourself a better night's sleep. When you eat just before going to bed, the digestive process is still in high gear, making you sleep less deeply, not to mention that you don't give yourself any time to burn off these calories.

15

GET
INFORMED

What follows is a crash course in nutrition. Eating healthily is the first step toward creating a healthy lifestyle. If you want to look good and feel good, take a break from those term papers and brush up on the science of food. Practice these principles and they will eventually become instinctual.

POP QUIZ

First, take this quick test to assess your diet plan. Then see how your responses compare with the "ideal" answers.

1. Do you eat breakfast? _____

2. How many meals a day do you eat out of a box (i.e., not freshly prepared)? _____

3. How many apple-sized servings of fruit do you eat daily? _____

4. How many handful-sized servings of veggies do you eat daily? _____

5. How many palm-sized servings of protein (meat, eggs, nuts) do you eat daily? _____

6. How many ounces of water do you drink daily?

7. How many hours do you work out per week? _____

1. Yes, I eat breakfast, even if it's only a piece of fruit on the way out the door. **2.** 1 or none; **3.** 3; **4.** 5; **5.** 2–3; **6.** Half of your body weight (in pounds) in ounces. For example, if you weigh 150 pounds, you should be drinking 75 ounces of water daily; **7.** 3–5 hours weekly.

DAPHNE'S BEST TIPS FOR IMPROVING HEALTH AND DIET

1. **DRINK HALF YOUR BODY WEIGHT IN OUNCES OF WATER DAILY,** including one glass before every meal. Drinking a full glass of water right before bed helps prevent bags under your eyes by flushing the salt out of your body that causes this swelling.

2. **AVOID EMOTIONAL EATING.** The next time you reach for that cookie, ask yourself whether you're being prompted by stress, hurt, depression, boredom, or even joy. The purpose of eating is to fuel the body.

3. **ALWAYS HAVE BREAKFAST.** It gives energy to your body and brain, and keeps you from going into starvation mode.

4. **SCHEDULE TIME EACH DAY TO EAT.** Plan on eating three meals and two snacks of fruits or veggies. Plan ahead by looking at your class schedule and establish when your windows of time are for meals. "Not enough time" is never an excuse.

5. COUNT TO YOUR AGE BEFORE YOU "CHEAT." Anytime you find you are about to eat something that would not be classified as healthy, take the time to count to your age. If you still want to have a bite after your countdown, feel free; you've made a conscious decision to indulge.

6. DITCH THE DEFEATIST ATTITUDE. Everyone falls off the bandwagon sometimes. The important thing is to get back on. So when you succumb to that late-night slice of pizza that your roommate just offered you, don't use this slip-up as an excuse to think, "Well, I've already been bad today, so I might as well finish the whole pie." Instead, enjoy the occasional indulgence and resume your resolve.

7. GET OFF THE COUCH. A daily exercise routine would be ideal. But, hey, even walking up a few flights of stairs for a face-to-face conversation would be a welcome improvement over instant-messaging.

8. AVOID PROCESSED SNACK FOODS. Always try to have a piece of fruit rather than a processed snack, especially late at night. If fruit alone doesn't cut it, try some peanut butter or low-fat cheese with it. If you really need a sugar fix, try dipping your fruit in a little melted chocolate.

ALL CALORIES ARE NOT CREATED EQUAL

Eating should be enjoyable—and you shouldn't have to feel deprived or count calories. To keep healthy and fit, though, you need to pick the right foods. Check out the lists on the following pages for your best food friends.

CARBOHYDRATE

Simple carbohydrates are made up almost entirely of refined, processed flour and sugar, and are to be avoided:

BAGELS	WHITE RICE
MUFFINS	DOUGHNUTS
BREAD STICKS	COOKIES & CAKES
WAFFLES	WHITE BREAD

Stick with complex carbohydrates like:

OATMEAL	BROWN RICE
WHOLE-GRAIN OR WHOLE WHEAT BREAD AND CRACKERS	GRANOLA BARS
	FARINA
	OAT BRAN

A FRUITS AND VEGGIES PRIMER

Fruits and vegetables are a great and satisfying source of the many vitamins and minerals you need to survive, not to mention look your best (the amino acids and nutrients in fruits improve your complexion and give you a radiant glow). They're also a terrific source of fiber, which fills you up and keeps you satisfied longer.

The Best Vegetables

SPINACH	BROCCOLI
KALE	CAULIFLOWER

The Best Fruits

APPLES	FIGS	ORANGES
APPLESAUCE, UNSWEETENED	GRAPEFRUIT	PAPAYA
	GRAPES	PEACHES
APRICOTS	KIWI	PEARS
BANANAS	LEMON	PINEAPPLE
BLACKBERRIES	LIME	PLUMS
BLUEBERRIES	MANGOES	RASPBERRIES
CHERRIES	MELON	STRAWBERRIES
CRANBERRIES	NECTARINES	

DO DAIRY

Lack of calcium and vitamin D can both stunt growth and make your bones weak. Getting this calcium is especially important since, according to *Time* magazine, the average teen gets 10 to 15 percent of her daily calories from soda, and carbonation can leach calcium out of bones. In this way, we are putting ourselves at unnecessary risk for osteoporosis, or bone thinning. (Trust me, this is one place you don't want to be thin.) That can of soda doesn't seem so refreshing now, does it?

GOT MILK?

Lean dairy foods, such as low-fat or fat-free varieties, offer a slew of benefits to the body. Along with other dairy products such as yogurt, cheese—even low-fat, sugar-free ice cream—milk is a good source of vitamin D, calcium, and other bone-strengthening nutrients.

A LITTLE PROTEIN

Americans consume about five times as much protein as we need daily, but often it's the wrong type of protein—that is, protein that is accompanied by tons of fat: hamburgers, chicken nuggets, ham and cheese.

Still, eating enough of the right protein keeps your muscles strong and powerful and your basal metabolism high.

Lean Sources of Protein, aka Good Protein

LEAN MEATS	LEGUMES (LENTILS, PEAS, BEANS, PEANUTS)	WHOLE-GRAIN BREAD
FISH		
POULTRY		SKINLESS CHICKEN OR TURKEY BREAST
EGGS	TOFU	
LOW-FAT CHEESE	PEANUT BUTTER	POACHED OR HARD-BOILED EGG

High-fat Sources of Protein, aka Bad Protein

CHICKEN NUGGETS	BACON	REFRIED BEANS
FRIED SHRIMP	HAMBURGERS	SAUSAGE

THE SKINNY ON FATS

Shocking as it may sound, some fats are not only good for you, but are absolutely essential to proper brain function, good joint movement, lustrous hair, glowing skin, and shiny nails— not to mention pleasure in life and eating, since fats make things taste good. What you want to avoid are "partially hydrogenated" and "saturated" fats.

Try to get your consumption of good fats into balance by lowering your intake of vegetable oils (used in most processed, boxed goodies) and working olive oil, flaxseed oil, and/or cod liver oil into your diet.

Daphne's recommendations for sources of good fat

OILY FISH:
SALMON, MACKEREL,
SARDINES, TUNA

COD LIVER OIL

AVOCADOS

FLAXSEED OIL

OLIVE OIL

CANOLA OIL

NUTS & SEEDS

FIBER

Young women should be getting about 25 grams of fiber daily. You can easily get this amount in your diet by eating 5 servings of raw fruits and veggies and a bowl of high-fiber cereal (such as shredded wheat or raisin bran) daily. Complex carbs such as brown rice and whole-grain bread are also good sources of fiber.

High fiber is a great aid when you're trying to lose weight because it helps you feel full faster and stay full longer.

High-fiber foods I can add to my diet

SHREDDED WHEAT CEREAL

RAISIN BRAN CEREAL

BROWN RICE

WHOLE-GRAIN BREAD

WHOLE FRUITS

WHOLE WHEAT PASTA

OATMEAL

LEGUMES
(LENTILS, PEAS, BEANS, ALMONDS, PEANUTS)

ROOT VEGETABLES
(CARROTS, TURNIPS, POTATOES)

PORTIONS

So how much of each of these different food categories should you be eating daily?

Daily Serving Checklist

3   servings of complex carbs (palm size = 1 serving)

5–8   servings of fruits or veggies (1 handful = 1 serving)

2   servings of dairy (cheese: 1 golf ball = 1 serving; yogurt/milk: see package for serving size—usually 1 cup)

3   servings of protein (palm size = 1 serving)

2   servings of red meat WEEKLY (palm size = 1 serving)

2   servings of good fats (see packaging—usually 1 teaspoon)

DANGER ZONES

Okay, so now you're armed with some dos and don'ts for healthy eating. But what happens during those particularly tempting times in college life when the healthy alternatives just aren't that obvious? Read on . . .

The five biggest danger zones in college are:

1. Late-Night Studying
2. Tailgating and Sports Events
3. Parties and Other Campus Gatherings
4. Watching TV
5. Late-Night Talks

What's your biggest danger zone?

_____

DANGER ZONE #1:

MAKING THE DEADLINE— STUDYING FOR TESTS AND WRITING PAPERS

You're bored, you're tired . . . and you've lost faith in your ability to graph linear equations. And then you start thinking that a little indulgence might get your brain going again.

Game Plan to Avoid Disaster

Plan scheduled breaks during which you've already planned what to eat, and eat something every hour:

- ★ baby carrots
- ★ almonds
- ★ piece of fruit: grapefruit, apple, pear
- ★ small handful of semisweet chocolate chips
- ★ rice cakes or soy crisps

Bonus Tips

- ★ Emergen-C packets are effervescent, single-serving packets of energy. Just dump a packet into a glass of water and you have an incredibly energizing drink that gives you a high dose of vitamin C and other vitamins and minerals.

- ★ Intermittently take breaks to go to the bathroom and splash warm water five times and then cool water five times onto your face. You can also take a brisk walk or climb a few flights of stairs to get the blood circulating after a long sitting session.

DANGER ZONE #2:

TAILGATING AND SPORTS EVENTS

The pre-game party can be more fun than the game itself. It can also mean more food than you'd normally consume in an entire day.

Game Plan to Avoid Disaster

☆ Have a bunless hamburger or hot dog.

☆ Stay away from potato salad, creamy coleslaw, or anything else with a lot of mayonnaise and fat.

☆ Offer to bring some dessert for the tailgate and bring a fruit salad.

☆ Stick to water or diet soda and peanuts at games, or pack an apple in your bag before you go.

Bonus Tips

☆ Move around and get different views of the game from points around the stadium. That way, you're getting in some extra steps rather than sitting for three hours straight, so you can eat some of what you love and have something to do besides sitting and eating.

☆ Moderation is everything: half a burger with the bun instead of the whole thing; a small serving of potato salad rather than a heaping mountain; a handful of chips instead of half the bag.

DANGER ZONE #3:

PARTIES AND OTHER CAMPUS GATHERINGS

Maybe it's because it's not quite a meal, but we tend to forget that calories count even when you're not sitting down at the dinner table.

Game Plan to Avoid Disaster

★ Eat a piece of fruit before you go, to put something in your stomach. Add a protein to your fruit/fiber to really get rid of any craving. Try unsweetened peanut butter or low-fat cheese.

★ Position yourself away from the food table.

★ Arrive at the party chewing sugarless gum. It will keep your mouth moving (so you aren't tempted to eat), freshen your breath, and may also increase your metabolism.

★ Keep a cup of water or a low-sugar beverage in hand at all times so your hands feel like they're doing something. Also, drinking lots of fluid will keep you feeling full so you aren't tempted to stock up on the snacks.

Bonus Tip

★ Think about how great you look at this party because you've been doing so well with the Dorm Room Diet, and how you want to look even better at the next one.

DANGER ZONE #4:

WATCHING TV

There's something about the guilty pleasure of watching TV that invites the guilty pleasure of junk food.

Game Plan to Avoid Disaster

★ Drink a glass of water before you have anything to eat; it often staves off cravings.

★ Chew gum.

★ Keep a bag of semisweet chocolate chips around, so if you want a sweet fix you can grab a small handful.

★ Try rice cakes or soy crisps before turning to more processed snacks; they come in a variety of flavors and the soy crisps even give you some protein.

Bonus Tips

★ Dip some fruit in chocolate and refrigerate it ahead of time.

★ Have some fresh fruit with peanut butter or low-fat cheese.

DANGER ZONE #5:

LATE-NIGHT TALKS

Gab sessions in the wee hours of the night sometimes lead to sweet and salty cravings.

Game Plan to Avoid Disaster

⭐ If you're in your own room having these chats, make sure that it is free of unhealthy temptations.

⭐ Have some sparkling water with fruit juice as a sweet fix before you eat anything. The bubbles will fill you up and won't leave you feeling bloated from having carbs right before bed.

⭐ Have some berries. They take time to eat, come in small pieces, and are sweet enough to sometimes remove the need to eat less healthful alternatives.

Bonus Tip

⭐ If you do succumb, make sure you know exactly how much unhealthy stuff you're eating by measuring it into a bowl. No eating ice cream out of the carton!

Before we move on to the next component of the Dorm Room Diet—exercise—take a moment to clarify what your goals are, which particular foods you need to avoid or replace, and what steps you need to take to get and stay on the right track.

PLAN OF ACTION

_____

_____

_____

_____

_____

_____

_____

_____

And while you're running from class to dorm, dorm to gym, gym to dorm, dorm to party, party to party, party to dorm, don't forget to find ways to relax and de-stress!

GET DE-STRESSED

BREATHING...

MEDITATION...

MASSAGE AND REFLEXOLOGY...

AROMATHERAPY

Anything you like to do that slows you down, calms you down, and refreshes your spirit.

Things I Can Do to De-stress:

_____

_____

_____

_____

GET
MOVING

WHY IS EXERCISE SO IMPORTANT?

★ tones your muscles

★ helps control your appetite

★ enhances your immune system

★ boosts brain power

★ improves your mood

★ increases blood circulation so your skin gets all the nutrients it needs

★ makes you more alert and focused

★ helps your heart and lungs work more efficiently

★ gives you more energy

★ helps counter stress, anxiety, and depression

Still think you don't have time to exercise?

CREATING AN EXERCISE PLAN

To get a complete body workout, you need to vary the intensity and the type of workout.

So decide what you like and what you are willing to try. The choices are endless!

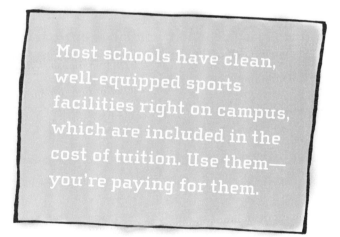

Most schools have clean, well-equipped sports facilities right on campus, which are included in the cost of tuition. Use them—you're paying for them.

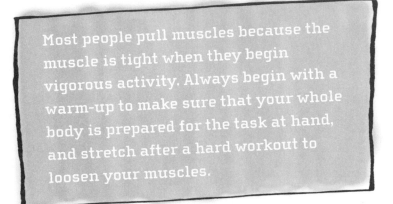

Most people pull muscles because the muscle is tight when they begin vigorous activity. Always begin with a warm-up to make sure that your whole body is prepared for the task at hand, and stretch after a hard workout to loosen your muscles.

With the Dorm Room Diet, you focus on your habits, not on counting calories. But some numbers do come in handy.

☆ On page 93 is a chart to help you determine whether you fall within a healthy weight range.

☆ Page 90 shows you how to calculate your basal metabolic rate—a personal formula for figuring out how many calories are just right for you.

☆ And page 92 tells you your target heart rate post-exercise.

BEFORE YOU START YOUR ROUTINE, BE SURE TO WARM UP:

- ★ Find a stairwell. Step up 2 steps with your right foot and bring your left foot to meet it. Step back down with your left foot first and bring your right foot to meet it. Alternate starting foot and repeat 60 times.

- ★ Roll your shoulders 10 times forward, 10 times backward, and then make 10 full circles with your arms out to the side, back 10 times and forward 10 times.

- ★ Swing your upper body in a circle by bending to the front, side, and back to rotate your hips 10 times in each direction.

- ★ Remember to breathe while you exercise!

On the pages that follow are some great exercise routines, complete with illustrations, that you can do right in your dorm room. Start slowly if you are new to this, and work up to the number of repetitions each exercise asks for. It's not a contest! The important thing is to get moving and keep moving.

There are logs to keep track of your progress starting on page 80.

Chest and Triceps

UPPER PUSH-UP Lie down on your stomach with palms down and shoulder-width apart. Push up and hold for 30 seconds. Keep your stomach pulled in to support your lower back.

LOWER PUSH-UP From push-up position, lower your body so that your chest is 6 inches off the floor and your back is straight. Hold for 30 seconds, then lower to the floor. Repeat 4 times.

CHEST STRETCH Sit on your heels, interweave your fingers behind your back, and lift your chest up 10 times by inhaling.

GIRL PUSH-UPS With your knees on the floor and ankles lifted and crossed. 20 push-ups.

CHAIR DIPS While holding yourself up in the position shown, walk your feet out in front of you until your legs are straight and you are resting on your palms and heels. Lift up with your arms and then lower 10 times. Hold the final dip for 30 seconds.

BACK STRETCH With right leg crossed over your left, twist your torso and try to place both hands on the back of the chair. Hold for 30 seconds. Repeat on the other side.

TRICEPS STRETCH Lift your right arm over your head, bending at the elbow as if to scratch the middle of your back. Press your right elbow down with your left palm until you feel a moderate stretch.

Do 10 more Chair Dips.

Reach across your chest with your right arm and bend your left arm at the elbow and use it to pull your right arm tight into your body. Repeat both stretches on the left side.

DOWN DOG INCLINE CHEST PUSH-UPS Start with your feet flat on the floor, and bend over to touch the floor. Put your palms flat on the floor (bend your knees if you need to) and walk your feet out behind you until you are in a pyramid position. Push your heels back so that you feel a stretch (not an ouch!) in the back of your thighs. You might need to come up onto your toes to relieve the stretch.

Slowly bring your body parallel to the floor by walking your feet backward. Bend your arms, keeping your elbows close to your sides, and lower your body about an inch off the floor. Hold for 5 seconds. Then go back to the down dog position by walking your feet forward again.

Repeat 10 times.

Legs

HUMAN CHAIR Press your back against a wall with your legs bent at a 90-degree angle. Hold this position for 1 minute. Keep your knees directly above your ankles.

TOE TOUCH Stand with your feet flat on the floor and bend at the waist; try to touch your toes. For a stronger stretch, lay your hands flat on the floor, palms down.

SIDE LEG LIFT Get down on all fours, knees shoulder-width apart. Lift your right leg out to the side as shown and then lower it. Repeat 50 times, and then 50 with your left leg.

BUTT STRETCH Sit down and put your feet as close to your butt as possible, slightly less than shoulder-width apart. Place your hands as shown and push your bottom a few inches up off the floor. Cross your right leg over your left knee, and lower your butt toward the floor to increase the stretch. Switch sides.

BACK KICK Flip back onto your hands and knees. With your knee bent, use your right butt cheek and pull the sole of your foot toward the ceiling, making a 45-degree angle. Repeat 50 times. Complete another 50 with your left leg.

STRAIGHT LEG STRETCH Sit on the floor and straighten your legs in front of you, ankles touching. Interlace your thumbs and lean forward and try to grip your feet. Hold for 20 seconds.

SIDE KNEE KICK Get back in the side lift position. This time, at the top of the lift extend the leg out to the side while tensing your leg muscles. Kick 5 times. Repeat with the other leg.

HALF BUTTERFLY TOE TOUCH While sitting, bend your right knee and pull your heel into your body while extending your left leg, pointing your toes toward the ceiling. Lean forward and touch your toes with your left hand. Hold for 30 seconds. Switch sides.

INNER LEG LIFT Lie on your right side and bend your left leg over your right leg, with your left foot flat on the floor. Hold your ankle with your left hand. Come up onto your right elbow to support your body. Lift your right leg 50 times, keeping the foot perpendicular to the leg (not pointing). Switch sides and do another 50.

LEG LIFT Sit with your legs in front of you. Bend your left leg up and interweave your fingers on the opposite side of that knee. Take the right leg with foot flexed and pointed straight up and lift it 6 inches off the floor. Tap the floor and come back up 50 times. Repeat with left leg.

BUTTERFLY Sit down and bring the flats of your feet together. Pull your heels as close in to your body as you can, while keeping your knees close to the floor. Hold for 30 seconds, elongating your spine.

LUNGES Stand upright, hands on hips. Step 2 feet in front of you with your right foot and bend both knees. Come back to standing position by pushing up with your thighs and bringing your right foot back to starting position. Alternate left and right leg until you have completed 50 lunges, being sure to keep the forward knee directly over the ankle.

QUAD PULL Standing upright, bend your right leg and grasp your ankle behind your back with both hands. Hold for 30 seconds and switch sides.

CALF LIFT Stand upright and, with toes pointing forward, lift up onto your toes. Come back to starting position. Repeat 25 times. Then point your toes in toward each other at about a 45-degree angle. Repeat the calf lift. Then face your toes out at a 45-degree angle, heels touching, and repeat. Then face your toes forward, lift your heels as high as you can, and hold for 30 seconds.

CALF STRETCH Lie on the floor. Climb your toes up a wall and place one foot as close to flat against the wall as you can. Lean into the wall to increase the stretch. Repeat with the other leg.

Back

LEG AND OPPOSITE ARM LIFT Kneeling on all fours, extend one leg and the opposite arm in opposite directions and hold for 1 minute. Switch sides.

BACK STRETCH Lie on your back, tuck your knees into your chest, and clasp your arms around your legs. Pull your knees in to your chest. Elongate your spine. Hold for 30 seconds.

HYPEREXTENSIONS Lie on your stomach with arms stretched in front of you. Arch your back and lift one leg and the opposite arm. Alternate 25 times. Rest for 10 seconds. Repeat twice.

LEG PULLS Lie on your stomach, bend your knees, and grasp both ankles with your hands. Use your leg strength and slowly lift your shoulders off the floor by pushing your legs back. Hold for 30 seconds.

THE TWIST On all fours, do the same motion as the leg and opposite arm lift but after extending in opposite directions, bring them back in to your body so the elbow and kneecap gently tap and then extend again. Repeat 25 times and switch sides.

BACK STRETCH Lying on your back, grab one knee with the opposite arm and bring it across your body while keeping your chest open by extending the other arm in the opposite direction. Breathe and sink down into the mat. Switch sides.

Shoulders and Biceps

TENNIS BALL TWISTS Stand up tall and stretch your arms out in front of you, making sure to keep your shoulders from rising up. Keep your neck long and shoulders down throughout the shoulder exercises. Pull your stomach in and slightly bend your knees. Curl your tailbone in and tighten your butt. Clench your hands as if gripping a tennis ball (or actually grab two, if you have them). While tensing your hands, twist them outward and then inward for 1 minute.

PALMS-UP CROSS Unclench your hands and face your palms up. Cross your hands back and forth over and under each other at a moderate pace for 1 minute.

PALMS-DOWN CROSS Face your palms down and repeat the previous exercise for 1 minute.

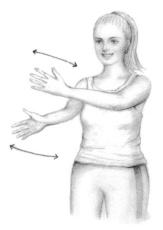

PALMS-IN CROSS Turn your palms toward each other and cross them over and under each other for 1 minute.

RELEASE AND ROLL SHOULDERS Drop your hands to your sides and rotate your shoulders in small circles, 10 times backward and 10 times forward.

ELBOWS TOGETHER Standing upright with your shoulders down, bend your arms at the elbows and bring your elbows together so that your palms and forearms are touching and your fingers are pointing to the ceiling. In this position, lift your arms 1 inch up and 1 inch down for 2 minutes.

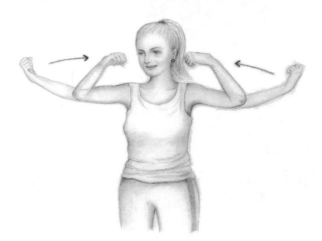

BICEPS CURLS Pretend you are holding dumbbells and stand with your arms out to either side of your body and bent at the elbow, so your elbows are even with your shoulders. Tense your arm muscles and extend your arms and then bring them back to upright position 60 times.

BUTT LIFT Sit down, extend your legs in front of you, and place your palms face down at your sides. Lift your body up and hold for 1 minute. Rest for 15 seconds, and repeat twice.

ARM BALANCE Sit cross-legged, place your palms face down at your sides, and lift your body off the floor for 10 seconds. Rest 10 seconds, and repeat 3 times.

SHOULDER STRETCH Sit with your legs extended in front of you. Grasp your right leg with your left arm and look over your right shoulder. Hold for 30 seconds and switch sides.

ABDOMINALS

Lower Abs

KNEES BENT LIFT Lying on your back with your arms folded across your chest, knees bent and feet flat on the floor, use your abs to lift your knees to your chest 30 times.

LEGS STRAIGHT UP Lie on your back with your legs straight up in the air and your feet flexed so they are parallel to your body. Interlock your thumbs and reach up to touch your toes 30 times.

BUTT LIFT In the same position, lift your butt 1 inch off the floor. Lift your heels straight up toward the ceiling 30 times. Then combine, lifting your upper body and tailbone simultaneously. Aim to get your tailbone about an inch off the floor with each lift. Repeat 30 times.

ONE LEG UP, ONE LEG DOWN Lie flat on your back with your body stretched stiff like a board and arms crossed over your chest. Keep one leg elongated on the floor and raise the other one so that it is perpendicular to the floor (stretched straight up). Bring the raised leg back down to the floor and lift the other leg up simultaneously. Alternate 20 times.

Obliques

SCISSOR KICKS Lie on your back and lift your outstretched legs between 6 inches and 1 foot off the floor. Extend your toes and cross your legs back and forth across each other 20 times. Then hold your extended leg 1 inch off the floor for 15 seconds. Repeat.

CIRCLES Lie on your back with your knees bent and feet on the floor; interweave your hands behind your head. Keep your lower back flat and circle your upper body up to the right, then cross over to the left and circle back down to the mat 20 times. Look up toward the ceiling the whole time. Reverse, starting with the left side, 20 times. Repeat both sides.

SIDE CRUNCHES Lie on your back with your fingers interlaced behind your head. Bend your knees and bring your legs to one side of your body by twisting your torso. If you're twisting to the left, your left leg should be resting on the floor, your knee bent at a 90-degree angle and your upper body and calves as close to parallel as possible. Use your abs to bring your upper body up in a crunch and back to the floor 30 times. Switch sides and repeat. Take a 30-second break and repeat both sides twice.

CROSSED LEG LIFT Turn to your side and lift your torso up with your arms while you extend your legs above the floor. Scissor your legs in the air at an angle 20 times. Switch sides and repeat.

Upper Abdominals

ONE LEG UP, REACH FOR TOE Lie on your back and make a "mountain" with one leg by bending the knee and keeping your foot flat on the floor. Bring your other leg straight up, perpendicular to your chest, and point your toes. Link your thumbs and straighten your arms in front of your body. Lift your upper body as high as you can off the floor. Return to resting position and repeat 20 times, then repeat on the other side.

45-DEGREE ANGLE LIFT TOWARD TOE Bend one knee and rest the opposite ankle on it. Place your hands behind your head and lift opposite elbow to opposite knee. Repeat 20 times, then do the other side.

CROSS-LEG SHOULDER TWIST Lie on your back with one leg extended up toward the ceiling and the other bent and crossed over it. Rest one arm comfortably across your chest or stomach and lightly clasp the back of your neck with the other hand. Lift your bent elbow to opposite knee 20 times. Repeat on the other side.

CROSSED LEG LIFT Turn on your side and lift your torso up with your arms while you extend your legs out above the floor. Lift the leg that is closest to the floor in small upward kicks toward the ceiling, in front of the other leg. Repeat 20 times. Repeat on the other side.

CROSSED ARMS BEHIND HEAD Lying on your back with your feet flat and knees up, cross your arms behind your head, making an X, but putting your opposite palm to opposite shoulder. Rest your head in the X. Use your abs to lift your upper body off the floor, looking up, and crunch your abs and lower 3 times. Repeat.

Midsection

PLANK HOLD Lie on your stomach and raise your straightened body off the floor onto your toes and forearms. Pull your stomach in. Hold for 1 minute.

SIDE PLANK In the plank position, turn away from the floor to face the wall. Place your weight onto your forearm, and hold for 1 minute.

REGULAR CRUNCHES Lie on your back and make "mountains" with your legs by bending the knees and keeping your feet flat on the floor. Interlace your fingers and gently clasp the back of your neck. Use your abs to lift your upper body halfway up to your knees and then back down to the floor and back up to the halfway position. Repeat 40 times, and hold that last crunch in the uppermost position for 1 minute.

KNEE LIFTS Standing up, bend your arms and bring clenched fists or opened palms toward your face. Lift your left knee to meet your left elbow. Bring your left foot back to the floor and lift your right knee to meet your right elbow. Alternate 20 times with each side. Repeat twice.

DORM ROOM DIET TIP

Falling off the exercise wagon (say, when your life is insane around finals time) does not mean your exercise routine is as good as dead. Just pick up where you left off as soon as you can.

CHEST AND TRICEPS
Log of Reps

	1st Workout	2nd Workout	3rd Workout	4th Workout
Upper Push-up	_____	_____	_____	_____
Lower Push-up	_____	_____	_____	_____
Chest Stretch	_____	_____	_____	_____
Girl Push-ups	_____	_____	_____	_____
Chair Dips	_____	_____	_____	_____
Back Stretch	_____	_____	_____	_____
Triceps Stretch	_____	_____	_____	_____
Down Dog Incline Chest Push-ups	_____	_____	_____	_____

LEGS

Log of Reps

	1st Workout	2nd Workout	3rd Workout	4th Workout
Human Chair	_____	_____	_____	_____
Toe Touch	_____	_____	_____	_____
Side Leg Lift	_____	_____	_____	_____
Butt Stretch	_____	_____	_____	_____
Back Kick	_____	_____	_____	_____
Straight Leg Stretch	_____	_____	_____	_____
Side Knee Kick	_____	_____	_____	_____
Half Butterfly Toe Touch	_____	_____	_____	_____
Inner Leg Lift	_____	_____	_____	_____
Leg Lift	_____	_____	_____	_____
Butterfly	_____	_____	_____	_____
Lunges	_____	_____	_____	_____
Quad Pull	_____	_____	_____	_____
Calf Lift	_____	_____	_____	_____
Calf Stretch	_____	_____	_____	_____

BACK

Log of Reps

	1st Workout	2nd Workout	3rd Workout	4th Workout
Leg and Opposite Arm Lift	_____	_____	_____	_____
Back Stretch	_____	_____	_____	_____
Hyperextensions	_____	_____	_____	_____
Leg Pulls	_____	_____	_____	_____
The Twist	_____	_____	_____	_____
Back Stretch	_____	_____	_____	_____

SHOULDERS AND BICEPS

Log of Reps

	1st Workout	2nd Workout	3rd Workout	4th Workout
Tennis Ball Twists	_____	_____	_____	_____
Palms-Up Cross	_____	_____	_____	_____
Palms-Down Cross	_____	_____	_____	_____
Palms-In Cross	_____	_____	_____	_____
Release and Roll Shoulders	_____	_____	_____	_____
Elbows Together	_____	_____	_____	_____
Biceps Curls	_____	_____	_____	_____
Butt Lift	_____	_____	_____	_____
Arm Balance	_____	_____	_____	_____
Shoulder Stretch	_____	_____	_____	_____

ABDOMINALS

Log of Reps

	1st Workout	2nd Workout	3rd Workout	4th Workout
Knees Bent Lift	_____	_____	_____	_____
Legs Straight Up	_____	_____	_____	_____
Butt Lift	_____	_____	_____	_____
One Leg Up, One Leg Down	_____	_____	_____	_____
Scissor Kicks	_____	_____	_____	_____
Circles	_____	_____	_____	_____
Side Crunches	_____	_____	_____	_____
Crossed Leg Lift	_____	_____	_____	_____
One Leg Up, Reach for Toe	_____	_____	_____	_____
45-degree Angle Lift Toward Toe	_____	_____	_____	_____
Cross-Leg Shoulder Twist	_____	_____	_____	_____
Crossed Leg Lift	_____	_____	_____	_____
Crossed Arms Behind Head	_____	_____	_____	_____

MIDSECTION
Log of Reps

	1st Workout	2nd Workout	3rd Workout	4th Workout
Plank Hold	_____	_____	_____	_____
Side Plank	_____	_____	_____	_____
Regular Crunches	_____	_____	_____	_____
Knee Lifts	_____	_____	_____	_____

GET THE
NUMBERS

Get Your Vitamins

The standard American diet—SAD—cries out for supplementation. The facing page shows the recommended daily amounts of vitamins and minerals.

Women between the ages of fifteen and twenty-five can follow this Basic Supplement Plan:

★ MULTIVITAMIN 1 tablet daily (try Solgar's Formula VM-75 with iron, for menstruating women, or Country Life's Daily Multi-Sorb)

★ ANTIOXIDANTS: VITAMINS C AND E Vitamin C with bioflavonoids, 500 milligrams daily (try Natrol's Ester-C or Twinlab's C-Plus Citrus Bioflavonoid Caps); vitamin E, 400 international units (try Twinlab's Super E-Complex, from mixed tocopherols)

★ MINERALS You'll get plenty of calcium, magnesium, zinc, and selenium from 2 capsules, 2 times daily of a multimineral vitamin. (Try Twinlab's Cellmins Multi Minerals; also found in multivitamins with minerals)

★ ESSENTIAL FATTY ACIDS 3 softgels daily (try Health from the Sun's The Total EFA, or, if you're a vegetarian, try 1 tablespoon of flaxseed oil, either mixed into salad dressing or taken straight)

RDA: Vitamins and Minerals

COMPOUND	ADULT FEMALES
Vitamin A (daily RE)	800
Vitamin D (daily IU)	200
Vitamin E (daily mg alpha TE)	8
Vitamin K (daily mcg)	65
Vitamin C (daily mg)	60
Folate (daily mcg)	400
Thiamin (B1) (daily mg)	1.1
Riboflavin (B2) (daily mg)	1.1
Niacin (daily mg)	14
Pyridoxine (B6) daily mg)	1.3
Cyanocobalamine (B12) (daily mcg)	2.4
Biotin (daily mcg)	30
Pantothenic Acid (daily mg)	5
Choline (daily mg)	425
Calcium (Ca) (daily mg)	1,000
Phosphorus (P) (daily mg)	700
Iodine (I) (daily mcg)	150

COMPOUND	ADULT FEMALES
Iron (Fe) (daily mg)	15
Magnesium (Mg) (daily mg)	320
Copper (Cu) (daily mg)	1.5–3
Zinc (Zn) (daily mg)	12
Selenium (Se) (daily mcg)	55
Chromium (Cr) (daily mcg)	50–200
Molybdenum (Mo) (daily mcg)	75–250
Manganese (Mn) (daily mg)	2–5
Fluoride (F) (daily mg)	3.0
Sodium (Na) (daily mg)	500
Chloride (Cl) (daily mg)	750
Potassium (K) (daily mg)	2,000

g = grams
mg = milligrams (0.001 g)
mcg = micrograms (0.000001 g)
IU = International Units
RE = Retinol Equivalent (1 RE = 3.33 IU vit A
    or 6 mcg beta carotene)
Alpha TE = Alpha Tocopherol Equivalent

The Harris-Benedict Formula for figuring out your Basal Metabolic Rate (BMR)

What's your number? Your BMR is the number of calories your body burns daily just to perform the basic functions of life. Here's the formula:

MEN: BMR = 66 + (6.23 x weight in pounds) + (12.7 x height in inches) − (6.8 x age in years)

WOMEN: BMR = 655 + (4.35 x weight in pounds) + (4.7 x height in inches) − (4.7 x age in years)

Example:

You are female
You are 19 years old
You weigh 130 pounds
You are 5'6" tall
Your BMR = 655 + 565 + 310 − 89 = 1441 calories/day

Activity Multiplier

Exercise burns calories and helps raise your BMR. So your caloric needs will change depending on your level of activity.

SEDENTARY = BMR x 1.2 (little or no exercise, sitting, driving, reading, sleeping)

LIGHT ACTIVITY = BMR x 1.375 (light exercise, walking, working out 1–3 days/week)

MODERATELY ACTIVE = BMR x 1.55 (moderate exercise/working out 1hr+, 3–5 days/week)

VERY ACTIVE = BMR x 1.725 (hard exercise/working out 1hr+, 6–7 days/week)

EXTREMELY ACTIVE = BMR x 1.9 (sports practice or a physical job, or working out 1hr+, twice daily)

Example:

Your BMR is 1441 calories per day
Your activity level is moderately active (work out 3–4 times per week)
Your activity factor is 1.55
Your Total Energy Needs = 1.55 x 1441 = 2233 calories/day

CALCULATING YOUR
TARGET HEART RATE RANGE

To determine your target heart rate, subtract your age from 220, then take this number and multiply by 0.6. This is your low limit. Then take the original 220 minus your age number and multiply by 0.85. This is your high limit. At the most intense part of your workout, your heart rate should fall somewhere between these numbers, but never above. When your heart rate exceeds this ideal range, your body switches from aerobic (your body is using oxygen to fuel metabolism to get energy) to anaerobic (your body is using other chemical processes that do not require oxygen to fuel cells— i.e., muscle contractions) exercising, meaning that the cells in your body have switched the source of their energy and will now fatigue faster because anaerobic activity produces waste molecules that impair activity and may make you unable to burn fat as quickly. So, if your heart rate rises above the high limit, slow down.

To figure out what your heart rate is at any given time, place your pointer and middle fingers on your opposite wrist or on your neck, an inch below your ear, so that you can feel your heartbeat. Count the number of beats in fifteen seconds and multiply that number by 4.

WHERE DO YOU FIT ON THIS CHART? These widely used weight ranges are based on Metropolitan Life Insurance Company tables that were developed from figures on low mortality rates, not necessarily optimum health. Therefore, you should aim for the lower to middle region within these ranges, as this is a more accurate reflection of a healthy weight for your height and build. Another easy way to determine the lower end of the range is that a five-foot-tall woman should weigh 100 pounds; add 5 pounds for each additional inch over five feet.

Weight Chart for Women

Height	Small Frame	Medium Frame	Large Frame
4'10"	100–110	100–120	117–131
4'11"	101–112	110–123	119–134
5'0"	103–115	112–126	122–137
5'1"	105–118	115–129	125–140
5'2"	108–121	118–132	128–144
5'3"	111–124	121–135	131–148
5'4"	114–127	124–138	134–152
5'5"	117–130	127–141	137–156
5'6"	120–133	130–144	140–160
5'7"	123–136	133–147	143–164
5'8"	126–139	136–150	146–167
5'9"	129–142	139–153	149–170
5'10"	132–145	142–156	152–173
5'11"	135–148	145–159	155–176
6'0"	138–151	148–162	158–179

GET
GOING
[JOURNAL PAGES]

OKAY, IT'S TIME TO PUT ALL THIS GOOD KNOWLEDGE to work for you. Use the pages that follow to keep track of your success (and, yes, occasional slip-ups).

Some people find it helpful to use a food and exercise diary daily. If that works for you, great! But don't beat yourself up if you sometimes skip it. Using it for three-to-five-day stretches is often all it takes to pick up any patterns you want to eliminate.

It's been my pleasure to share with you what insight I've gained over my years living independently at college. Remember that independence is all about choice: You can *choose* to live healthfully. So take care of yourself. Use your new adult independence to take responsibility for your health and your life now!

TIP OF THE DAY

When people are trying to lower their fat intake, they often swap margarine for butter. This is not a good choice because margarine contains hydrogenated fats, the kind that will stick to the lining of your various tubes, especially those in and around your heart, which can lead to artery clogs later in life. The better plan is to just eat butter sparingly.

Thing I'm glad I ate:

_____

_____

_____

_____

_____

Things I'd like to forget I ate:

_____

_____

_____

_____

_____

What I drank:

What I'd like to forget I drank:

_____

_____

_____

_____

_____

_____

_____

_____

_____

_____

My workout included:

_____

_____

My overall mood/stress level today was:

_____

_____

DATE: _____

TIP OF THE DAY

You can avoid snacking from the vending machines by stashing healthful nonperishable foods on your shelf. Think nuts, dried fruit, popcorn, and cereal bars. Don't go overboard or the temptation to snack on autopilot could be overwhelming.

Thing I'm glad I ate:

_____

_____

_____

_____

_____

Things I'd like to forget I ate:

_____

_____

_____

_____

_____

What I drank:

_____

_____

_____

_____

_____

What I'd like to forget I drank:

_____

_____

_____

_____

_____

My workout included:

_____

_____

My overall mood/stress level today was:

_____

_____

DATE: _____

TIP OF THE DAY

Make your own salad dressing in the cafeteria,
to avoid all the sugars in bottled dressings.
Just stir together olive oil, balsamic vinegar, a
dash of soy sauce, and a teaspoon of mustard.

Thing I'm glad I ate:

Things I'd like to forget I ate:

_____

_____

_____

_____

_____

_____

_____

_____

_____

_____

_____

_____

What I drank: What I'd like to forget I drank:

_____   _____

_____   _____

_____   _____

_____   _____

_____   _____

My workout included:

_____

_____

My overall mood/stress level today was:

_____

_____

DATE: _____

TIP OF THE DAY

If you overindulge today, eat healthfully tomorrow and the next day. Experts agree that caloric intake should be measured over a period of several days, not just one meal.

Thing I'm glad I ate:

_____

_____

_____

_____

_____

Things I'd like to forget I ate:

_____

_____

_____

_____

_____

What I drank:

_____

_____

_____

_____

_____

What I'd like to forget I drank:

_____

_____

_____

_____

_____

My workout included:

_____

_____

My overall mood/stress level today was:

_____

_____

DATE: _____

TIP OF THE DAY

Watch for the words "sugar added" (usually in small type) on bottles of fruit juice. They can have as much sugar in them as a can of soda. And beware of the terms "juice drink" and "cocktail." Generally, these beverages contain low amounts of real fruit juice—as low as 5 percent.

Thing I'm glad I ate:

_____

_____

_____

_____

_____

_____

Things I'd like to forget I ate:

_____

_____

_____

_____

_____

_____

What I drank: What I'd like to forget I drank:

_____   _____

_____   _____

_____   _____

_____   _____

_____   _____

My workout included:

_____

_____

My overall mood/stress level today was:

_____

_____

DATE: _____

TIP OF THE DAY

Drizzle a little chocolate on a banana and stick it in the freezer overnight. Then when that ice cream craving hits, pull it out for a guiltless frozen treat.

Thing I'm glad I ate:

_____

_____

_____

_____

_____

Things I'd like to forget I ate:

_____

_____

_____

_____

_____

What I drank:

What I'd like to forget I drank:

_____

_____

_____

_____

_____

_____

_____

_____

_____

_____

My workout included:

_____

_____

My overall mood/stress level today was:

_____

_____

DATE: _____

TIP OF THE DAY

Pop popcorn using an air popper, sprinkle with a little olive oil and a dash of salt, and you've got a crunchy low-fat snack.

Thing I'm glad I ate:

_____

_____

_____

_____

_____

_____

Things I'd like to forget I ate:

_____

_____

_____

_____

_____

_____

What I drank:

_____

_____

_____

_____

_____

What I'd like to forget I drank:

_____

_____

_____

_____

_____

My workout included:

_____

_____

My overall mood/stress level today was:

_____

_____

DATE: _____

TIP OF THE DAY

Fast food chains are potential minefields for the healthy eater. Even the salads can be troubling. Be wary of prepackaged dressings, as they're often loaded with sugars and extra calories. So check the nutrition label before dousing your salad.

Thing I'm glad I ate:

_____

_____

_____

_____

_____

Things I'd like to forget I ate:

_____

_____

_____

_____

_____

What I drank:

What I'd like to forget I drank:

_____

_____

_____

_____

_____

_____

_____

_____

_____

_____

My workout included:

_____

_____

My overall mood/stress level today was:

_____

_____

DATE: _____

TIP OF THE DAY

Exercise doesn't have to take two hours. It doesn't even have to take place in a gym. Walking to the library to study instead of staying in your dorm or taking the stairs instead of the elevator are excellent ways to work more movement into your day.

Thing I'm glad I ate:

_____

_____

_____

_____

_____

Things I'd like to forget I ate:

_____

_____

_____

_____

_____

What I drank:

_____

_____

_____

_____

_____

What I'd like to forget I drank:

_____

_____

_____

_____

_____

My workout included:

_____

_____

My overall mood/stress level today was:

_____

_____

DATE: _____

TIP OF THE DAY

Vitamin and mineral supplements can help make up for the nutrients you don't get from the food you eat. They're like an insurance policy. However, they are not a substitute for a nutritious diet.

Thing I'm glad I ate:

_____

_____

_____

_____

_____

_____

Things I'd like to forget I ate:

_____

_____

_____

_____

_____

_____

What I drank:

What I'd like to forget I drank:

_____

_____

_____

_____

_____

_____

_____

_____

_____

_____

My workout included:

_____

_____

My overall mood/stress level today was:

_____

_____

DATE: _____

TIP OF THE DAY

Conservative estimates show that after puberty, 5 to 10 percent of American women are living with some form of eating disorder. Attempting to use your diet to control your weight is one thing. Engaging in hazardous undereating is potentially lethal and should be reported to a professional.

Thing I'm glad I ate:

_____

_____

_____

_____

_____

_____

Things I'd like to forget I ate:

_____

_____

_____

_____

_____

_____

What I drank: What I'd like to forget I drank:

_____   _____

_____   _____

_____   _____

_____   _____

_____   _____

My workout included:

_____

_____

My overall mood/stress level today was:

_____

_____

DATE: _____

TIP OF THE DAY

Thirst sometimes masquerades as hunger. Drink a glass of water when a hunger pang hits. If you still feel hungry afterward, then it's the real thing.

Thing I'm glad I ate:

_____

_____

_____

_____

_____

Things I'd like to forget I ate:

_____

_____

_____

_____

_____

What I drank:

_____

_____

_____

_____

_____

What I'd like to forget I drank:

_____

_____

_____

_____

_____

My workout included:

_____

_____

My overall mood/stress level today was:

_____

_____

DATE: _____

TIP OF THE DAY

Forget about calorie counting because that number is going to vary based on your metabolism and how much exercise you are getting. Instead, listen to your body and eat when you're hungry. If you find that it's too much or not enough food for your body type, adjust accordingly.

Thing I'm glad I ate:

_____

_____

_____

_____

_____

_____

Things I'd like to forget I ate:

_____

_____

_____

_____

_____

_____

What I drank:

_____

_____

_____

_____

_____

What I'd like to forget I drank:

_____

_____

_____

_____

_____

My workout included:

_____

_____

My overall mood/stress level today was:

_____

_____

DATE: _____

TIP OF THE DAY

Some people assume that tortilla-wrapped sandwiches are better for you than regular sandwiches because there is "less bread." However, a tortilla is actually a more condensed form of carbohydrates and has twice as many calories as two pieces of whole-grain bread.

Thing I'm glad I ate:

_____

_____

_____

_____

_____

_____

Things I'd like to forget I ate:

_____

_____

_____

_____

_____

What I drank:

What I'd like to forget I drank:

_____

_____

_____

_____

_____

_____

_____

_____

_____

_____

My workout included:

_____

_____

My overall mood/stress level today was:

_____

_____

DATE: _____

TIP OF THE DAY

Try to avoid foods like nonfat ice cream or low-fat brownies. Chances are the manufacturers have put something in there to replace the fat, so you end up with extra sugar, salt, or some artificial creation that your body can't digest.

Thing I'm glad I ate:

_____

_____

_____

_____

_____

_____

Things I'd like to forget I ate:

_____

_____

_____

_____

_____

_____

What I drank:

_____

_____

_____

_____

_____

What I'd like to forget I drank:

_____

_____

_____

_____

_____

My workout included:

_____

_____

My overall mood/stress level today was:

_____

_____

DATE: _____

TIP OF THE DAY

If you must have pasta, opt for the whole wheat preparations. If that's not an option, go for regular pasta with a light tomato sauce. Marinara primavera and other sauces that are basically just tomatoes, vegetables, olive oil, and herbs are your best bet.

Thing I'm glad I ate:

_____

_____

_____

_____

_____

Things I'd like to forget I ate:

_____

_____

_____

_____

_____

What I drank:

_____

_____

_____

_____

_____

What I'd like to forget I drank:

_____

_____

_____

_____

_____

My workout included:

_____

_____

My overall mood/stress level today was:

_____

_____

DATE: _____

TIP OF THE DAY

Fruit leathers are a great sweet snack with one-quarter the calories of a candy bar.

Thing I'm glad I ate:

_____

_____

_____

_____

_____

_____

Things I'd like to forget I ate:

_____

_____

_____

_____

_____

_____

What I drank:

_____

_____

_____

_____

_____

What I'd like to forget I drank:

_____

_____

_____

_____

_____

My workout included:

_____

_____

My overall mood/stress level today was:

_____

_____

DATE: _____

Thing I'm glad I ate:

_____

_____

_____

_____

_____

_____

Things I'd like to forget I ate:

_____

_____

_____

_____

_____

_____

What I drank:

_____

_____

_____

_____

_____

What I'd like to forget I drank:

_____

_____

_____

_____

_____

My workout included:

_____

_____

My overall mood/stress level today was:

_____

_____

DATE: _____

TIP OF THE DAY

Standing in front of the refrigerator and digging a spoon into a carton of ice cream just makes you feel fat and slovenly. If you're going to indulge in high-fat food, serve yourself a small portion in a small, attractive dish. Then sit down and enjoy it slowly so you feel satisfied.

Thing I'm glad I ate:

_____

_____

_____

_____

_____

_____

Things I'd like to forget I ate:

_____

_____

_____

_____

_____

_____

What I drank: What I'd like to forget I drank:

_____   _____

_____   _____

_____   _____

_____   _____

_____   _____

My workout included:

_____

_____

My overall mood/stress level today was:

_____

_____

DATE: _____

Find ways to enjoy the foods you can't live without, but do so in either smaller portions or combined with foods that will make it easier for you to say you're already full and mean it. For example, just about any fruit can be dipped in melted chocolate.

Thing I'm glad I ate:

_____

_____

_____

_____

_____

Things I'd like to forget I ate:

_____

_____

_____

_____

_____

What I drank: What I'd like to forget I drank:

_____   _____

_____   _____

_____   _____

_____   _____

_____   _____

My workout included:

_____

_____

My overall mood/stress level today was:

_____

_____

DATE: _____

TIP OF THE DAY

Add lemon juice and a little sugar to a bowl of cut-up fruit. It adds zest with minimal calories. Plus, lemon juice acts as an appetite suppressant.

Thing I'm glad I ate:

_____

_____

_____

_____

_____

Things I'd like to forget I ate:

_____

_____

_____

_____

_____

What I drank: What I'd like to forget I drank:

_____   _____

_____   _____

_____   _____

_____   _____

_____   _____

My workout included:

_____

_____

My overall mood/stress level today was:

_____

_____

DATE: _____

TIP OF THE DAY

Read the book *Fast Food Nation* by Eric Schlosser. You may never crave fast food again. (Yeah, it's that convincing.)

Thing I'm glad I ate:

_____

_____

_____

_____

_____

_____

Things I'd like to forget I ate:

_____

_____

_____

_____

_____

_____

What I drank:

_____

_____

_____

_____

_____

What I'd like to forget I drank:

_____

_____

_____

_____

_____

My workout included:

_____

_____

My overall mood/stress level today was:

_____

_____

DATE: _____

TIP OF THE DAY

In the long run, conventional diets will most likely cause you to gain weight, as it's only a matter of time before you go off them and binge your way through several forbidden items. And even if you do manage to stick to a tough program, who wants to be known as "that girl who can't eat anything"?

Thing I'm glad I ate:

_____

_____

_____

_____

_____

Things I'd like to forget I ate:

_____

_____

_____

_____

_____

What I drank:

_____

_____

_____

_____

_____

What I'd like to forget I drank:

_____

_____

_____

_____

_____

My workout included:

_____

_____

My overall mood/stress level today was:

_____

_____

DATE: _____

TIP OF THE DAY

When you're in the cafeteria, never ask anyone to just "grab" you something while she's up refilling her own plate. If there's something you want, get up and get it yourself. You'll be surprised how much laziness will keep you from eating something you don't really want or need.

Thing I'm glad I ate:

_____

_____

_____

_____

_____

Things I'd like to forget I ate:

_____

_____

_____

_____

_____

What I drank:

_____

_____

_____

_____

_____

What I'd like to forget I drank:

_____

_____

_____

_____

_____

My workout included:

_____

_____

My overall mood/stress level today was:

_____

_____

DATE: _____

TIP OF THE DAY

Have a small piece of fruit before going out to dinner. This will take the edge off your hunger and make you less likely to overeat.

Thing I'm glad I ate:

_____

_____

_____

_____

_____

Things I'd like to forget I ate:

_____

_____

_____

_____

_____

What I drank: What I'd like to forget I drank:

_____   _____

_____   _____

_____   _____

_____   _____

_____   _____

My workout included:

_____

_____

My overall mood/stress level today was:

_____

_____

DATE: _____

TIP OF THE DAY

If a road trip with friends lands you in the drive-through line at a fast-food restaurant, be prepared. It's probably not realistic to eat a salad on the road, so instead remember portion control. In other words, order the junior-sized burger rather than the big daddy. And when they ask if you want it with extra-special sauce, just say no.

Thing I'm glad I ate:

_____

_____

_____

_____

_____

_____

Things I'd like to forget I ate:

_____

_____

_____

_____

_____

_____

What I drank:

_____

_____

_____

_____

_____

What I'd like to forget I drank:

_____

_____

_____

_____

_____

My workout included:

_____

_____

My overall mood/stress level today was:

_____

_____

DATE: _____

TIP OF THE DAY

Any simple carbs you eat late at night end up as fat (since you won't be doing much exercising while you sleep), and sleeping on a full stomach invariably leaves you starving in the morning. So if you must have a late-night snack, eat something fibrous, so when you get up in the morning there will still be sugar circulating in your blood.

Thing I'm glad I ate:

_____

_____

_____

_____

_____

_____

Things I'd like to forget I ate:

_____

_____

_____

_____

_____

_____

What I drank:

What I'd like to forget I drank:

_____   _____

_____   _____

_____   _____

_____   _____

_____   _____

My workout included:

_____

_____

My overall mood/stress level today was:

_____

_____

DATE: _____

TIP OF THE DAY

Most college students are on a pretty tight budget. And processed foods do tend to be less expensive than fresh foods. But the cost of dealing with poor eating habits when you're older—future medical bills for everything from heart disease to diabetes to a shrink for your body-image issues—easily outweighs the relatively small price you pay today.

Thing I'm glad I ate:

_____

_____

_____

_____

_____

_____

Things I'd like to forget I ate:

_____

_____

_____

_____

_____

_____

What I drank: What I'd like to forget I drank:

_____   _____

_____   _____

_____   _____

_____   _____

_____   _____

My workout included:

_____

_____

My overall mood/stress level today was:

_____

_____

DATE: _____

TIP OF THE DAY

Always having breakfast ensures that your body won't go into starvation-preservation mode and also provides your body and brain with energy so you can be on top of your game.

Thing I'm glad I ate:

Things I'd like to forget I ate:

_____

_____

_____

_____

_____

_____

What I drank:

_____

_____

_____

_____

_____

What I'd like to forget I drank:

_____

_____

_____

_____

_____

My workout included:

_____

_____

My overall mood/stress level today was:

_____

_____

DATE: _____

TIP OF THE DAY

Plan on eating three meals and two snacks of fruits or veggies daily. Ideally, you'll want to nourish your body every three hours so you won't get ravenous and binge. So look at your class schedule and establish when your windows of time are for meals. "Not enough time" is never an excuse.

Thing I'm glad I ate:

_____

_____

_____

_____

_____

_____

Things I'd like to forget I ate:

_____

_____

_____

_____

_____

_____

What I drank:

_____

_____

_____

_____

_____

What I'd like to forget I drank:

_____

_____

_____

_____

_____

My workout included:

_____

_____

My overall mood/stress level today was:

_____

_____

DATE: _____

ABOUT THE AUTHOR

Daphne Oz, a student at Princeton University, grew up in Cliffside Park, New Jersey, with her three younger siblings, Arabella, Zoe, and Oliver. While still in high school she was a writer for *ELLEgirl* magazine, and she changed her school's lunch menu from processed cafeteria food to include whole grains and raw foods. The daughter of Lisa and Dr. Mehmet Oz, co-author of the bestsellers *You: The Owner's Manual, You: The Smart Patient,* and *You: On a Diet,* she is the author of *The Dorm Room Diet: The 8-Step Program for Creating a Healthy Lifestyle Plan That Really Works.*

THE DORM ROOM DIET books by Daphne Oz

THE DORM ROOM DIET: The 8-Step Program for Creating a Healthy Lifestyle Plan That Really Works

_____ copies at $16.95 each • Paperback • ISBN: 978-1-55704-685-7

Figuring out how to eat right and stay healthy on your own is hard! Here is help from someone who's been there. Daphne's 8-step program for looking good, feeling great, and staying fit shows you how to: stop eating out of emotional need • navigate the most common danger zones at school for unhealthy eating • get the exercise you need, even in your small dorm room • choose vitamins and supplements wisely • relax and rejuvenate amid the stress of college life.

THE DORM ROOM DIET PLANNER

_____ copies at $12.95 each • Paperback • ISBN: 978-1-55704-761-8

Based on the successful principles of Daphne's first book, this user-friendly companion guide is filled with motivational tips and checklists for you to keep track of your progress. _The Dorm Room Diet Planner_ also features a special journal section to help jump-start the first 30 days of your program.

For postage and handling, please add $5.00 for the first book, plus $1.50 for each additional book. Prices and availability are subject to change. Please call 800-669-3903 to place a credit card order. I enclose a check or money order payable to **Newmarket Press** in the amount of $ _____

Name _____

Address_____

City/State/Zip _____

E-mail Address _____

For discounts on orders of five or more copies or to get a catalog, contact Newmarket Press, Special Sales Department, 18 East 48th Street, New York, NY 10017; phone 212-832-3575 or 800-669-3903; fax 212-832-3629; or e-mail sales@newmarketpress.com
www.newmarketpress.com